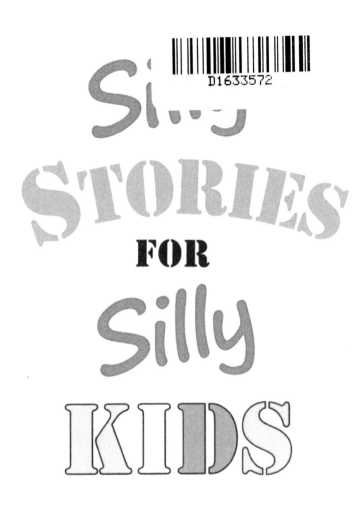

Silly
STORIES
FOR
Silly
KIDS

By
Silly Willy

Contents

My Super Hero Diary

Tuesday, February 26th

Dear Diary,

It's me again, **Captain Fantastic**. You know, the best superhero in the world.

Boy, what a day I had. No beating up bad guys or saving the world today, but still…

First, I woke up at 7am. I had some breakfast (cereal, orange juice, and plutonium—a balanced breakfast for any superhero), but we were out of milk. Again!

I think my roommate, Colonel Evilpants, keeps drinking it all on purpose, just to make me angry!

I went to the supermarket to get more milk, along with some other groceries—eggs, bread, toilet paper, and engine oil for the invisible jet.

But they were all out of milk!

I complained to the manager, but he just shrugged his shoulders and walked away.

This made me so mad that I did something I probably shouldn't have—I used my supersonic powers to make all the watermelons in the store explode. I felt bad, so I wrote a check to the manager and apologized.

Then, I went to the laundromat to do my laundry. I really get sweaty when I'm fighting bad guys, so I needed to wash all my superhero suits and my underwear. My clothes were drying when I thought I heard a scream outside. Was someone in trouble? Did they need Captain Fantastic to save them? I ran outside, but I only saw my roommate, Colonel Evilpants, rolling on the ground laughing at me. He was playing a joke on me again!

I went back into the laundromat and realized I had left my clothes in the dryer too long. Everything had shrunk! I tried on one of my superhero suits, and it split—right along my butt!

How embarrassing!

I ran out to my car, trying to hide the tear in my suit. But then my car wouldn't start! I scurried to the bus stop nearby and got on the bus.

Then, when I was walking towards a seat, I dropped my wallet and had to bend down to pick it up. My suit tore even more, and everyone could see my underwear. Some kids in the back started laughing at me. I was so embarrassed!

What a bad day!

Finally, I got home and ran inside to change. Whenever I'm feeling upset, nothing cheers me up like doing some gardening. I put on my pink gardening apron, my yellow gardening hat and my pink gardening gloves.

I went outside to tend to my daisies, tulips, and mutant Venus flytraps.

I was just starting to relax and to forget about my bad day when Colonel Evilpants' friends drove past and laughed at me. I don't know what's so funny about a superhero doing his gardening in his favorite garden apron and hat!

So that was my day, Diary. Maybe tomorrow I'll get to fight some bad guys...

The Pyramid!

Thousands of years ago in Egypt there was a builder. His name was **Hut-tut-nut** and he loved to build temples for the pharaoh.

One day, the pharaoh came to see him.

"Hut-tut-nut," he said, "Will you build me a pyramid? I want to have the biggest pyramid in the world."

The pharaoh drew a picture of the pyramid he wanted on a sheet of paper and gave it to Hut-tut-nut.

Hut-tut-nut was so excited! He ran to find his friends, and they began working right away.

They built the pyramid little by little. Finally, 17 years later, the pyramid was finished. Hut-tut-nut told the pharaoh to come see his amazing pyramid in the desert.

The pharaoh looked at the pyramid and became red with anger.

"**Hut-tut-nut!** My pyramid is built wrong!" he shouted.

Hut-tut-nut gulped. He was in trouble now!

"The pyramid is upside down!"

The Castle on the Hill!

Once upon a time, in a faraway land, there were castles everywhere. Everyone had a castle.

Some of the castles were big with moats.

One family couldn't afford a moat. Instead, they set up water sprinklers around their castle to keep out invaders.

Some of the castles were tall with gold towers, while one of the castles was so small that it only had one tiny window.

Some of the castles smelt nice like flowers.

But other castles stunk like rotten fish. **Ewww.**

One castle was guarded by a dragon.

Another family couldn't find a dragon, so they dressed up their dog in a dragon costume. (The dog couldn't breathe fire, but it had really stinky breath!)

In this faraway land, there also lived a young boy named Bobby Banana. Bobby wasn't a banana, but for some reason that was his last name. He always wondered if one of his great-great-great grandparents was a banana.

But that's not what this story is about…

Bobby had just turned 10, and it was time for him to move out of his parents' castle and build his own castle. In this faraway land, boys and girls were only allowed to live with their parents until they turned 10. If they didn't follow this rule, they would be forced to wash their parents' underwear forever. No one wanted to wash their parents' underwear!

Bobby packed up his things and walked around looking for a great place to build his castle. He didn't have a lot of money, but he wanted his castle to be as big as he could build it. He wanted everyone in town to be jealous of his castle!

Should he build his castle in the river? That would be new and different.

"No," he thought to himself. "That would be too wet."

Should he build his castle in the big, huge tree in the middle of town? That way, everyone would walk by his castle and admire it.

"No," he thought to himself again. "The birds and squirrels would always be sneaking in and stealing my dinner—acorns and bird food."

Bobby thought and he thought and he thought. Then, he suddenly said, "I've got it! I know where I can build my castle! Even though I don't have a lot of money, I could still have the tallest castle in the town. I'll build my castle on top of that hill!"

Bobby climbed up to the top of the hill and looked out over the town.

"I'm already higher than any other castle here," he said. "Even the king's castle is shorter than this hill. I'm going to have the best castle in town!"

Bobby began building his castle. It wasn't very big and it wasn't very tall, but it was taller than everyone else's since it was sitting on the hill.

Bobby was so excited about his castle that he rushed to build it as quickly as possible. He couldn't wait to show it off to his parents and his friends.

Finally, the castle was finished. It sat on the edge of the hill and looked down on the town. It was not very well built. It leaned over and looked wonky. But Bobby had plenty of flags on the castle. Each flag had Bobby's face on it. Bobby wanted to make sure everyone knew this was his castle.

Bobby ran down the hill to find his parents and his friends to show them his castle. He just reached the town when all of a sudden, he heard a loud crack. The sound echoed through the town, and everyone came outside to see what the noise was.

Bobby turned around just in time to see his castle swaying on the top of the hill before it tumbled down the hill towards the town!

Everyone screamed!

Bobby's castle was racing down the hill like a bowling ball and was heading straight for the town!

His castle was out of control. It
knocked down one castle, then another, then
another. It left a path of destroyed castles
behind it.

One of the villagers shouted out, "Hey! That runaway castle is destroying the whole village! Whose castle is that?"

"Oh no!" Bobby said to himself. "I'm going to get in soooooo much trouble! Wait, maybe they won't know it was my castle."

Another villager shouted, "Hey! I see something! What are those flags on the runaway castle?"

"Uh oh," Bobby said to himself, as he remembered that the flags had his face on them.

He heard one of the villagers call out, "Hey! That's Bobby Banana's face! Where is that little punk?"

"Time to run away!" Bobby snuck away from the crowd and ran as fast as he could. That's the day that Bobby Banana decided that castles just weren't for him.

Double Trouble!

Grace was very smart. Really, really smart. Especially for a 6 year old. But Grace did not like doing what she was told. She never followed the teacher's instructions at school. Nor would she obey her parents at home. She was always in trouble for disobeying commands. Then Grace thought of a brilliant plan.

She would make a copy of herself to obey everyone's commands while she went about doing whatever she liked.

Grace stayed up all night, using her big brain to build a copying machine! Early one morning she finished, but it needed testing. The first thing she copied was herself! Pop! It worked! Two Graces! Grace now had a clone of herself! "I'm a genius!" yelled Grace...and Grace! **They were absolutely identical!**

However, she soon discovered a problem.

The new clone of Grace, just like the original, did not obey orders! Now, there was no housework completed. In fact, it got messier twice as quick with two Graces!

Picky, Picky, Picky!

There was a boy who loved to pick his nose. He always picked his nose. At the table, he would pick his nose. On the bus, he would pick his nose. At school, he would pick his nose. He could pick his nose with any of his fingers. He could also pick his nose with any of his toes! He was not popular with anyone because of his nose picking.

One time his fingers got stuck in his nose, so he blew them out with a sneeze!

Gross.

He offered to pick other people's noses, but no one ever accepted his offer. He even offered an elephant a trunk pick.

But the elephant didn't want his trunk picked either. He wanted to enter nose picking competitions, but they did not exist.

One day picking your nose became very cool! Everybody wanted to be seen picking their nose. As he was so good at picking his nose the boy became famous overnight! His face was everywhere, he was famous! The boy was featured in magazines and TV shows.

He even appeared on the sides of buses picking his nose. Suddenly he had the attention of girls! All the girls wanted the nose picking boy to be their boyfriend. "Pick my nose, pick my nose," the girls would scream to him. But he could not decide who should be his girlfriend— he was too picky!

The Mystery Stink!

Hi, my name is Tom. I'm eight years old and I live in a house in the suburbs. That's me in the picture.

The guy beside me there is Jack. He's my best friend. We do everything together — we ride our bikes, we play in the woods, and we play video games. Sometimes, we even solve mysteries together.

One day, we were hanging out in my room. All of a sudden...Sniff sniff.

"What's that?" I said. "Something REALLY stinks!"

Sniff sniff. "I smell it, too!" said Jack. "Yuck! What is it?"

We went to the kitchen.

"Maybe it's the meatloaf my mom cooked last night," I said. "It always smells a bit stinky."

We searched the fridge. No stinky meatloaf in there.

"Where is it coming from?"

We walked to my older sister's room. Normally, I'm not allowed in her room, but this was an emergency. A stinky emergency!

"My sister's got perfume and lotion that stinks," I said. "Maybe it's in here."

We searched her whole room — under her bed, in her dresser, in her closet, even in her secret diary. (Shhh... don't tell! She'll kill me!) There was nothing! We searched around the house but couldn't find the cause of the smell.

"Yuck!" I said, "The smell is getting worse! It smells like a twenty-year-old rotten egg!"

"It smells like my baby brother's diapers!" Jack replied.

I had one more idea. We went to the back door.

"Maybe the smell is outside," I said. "Maybe it's dog poo or some stinky animal in the woods."

We searched and searched and searched the yard. Nothing. Just an unstinky dog and some unstinky birds and squirrels.

"I give up!" I said. "I can't find this smell anywhere!"

We headed back into the house and I took off my shoes.

"Yuck!" said Jack. "The smell is stronger!"

He paused.

"Wait... it's your feet! Gross! They smell like a skunk's house after a big skunk party!"

"Ah ha!" I shouted.

"We solved the case of the Mystery Stink! But we need to be sure..."

I rubbed my feet in his face... you know, just to be sure!

Maximum Whoops!

Max is a man with a dog, also named Max. Max wanted an adventure, so he booked a holiday through a travel agent. Max told the travel agent he wanted to be surprised for his holiday.

However, he did not have much money to spend.

The travel agent said that this was possible, but he wouldn't be able to take Max, the dog, with him.

The travel agent said that he would arrange accommodation for Max, the dog. The travel agent gave both Max and Max sealed envelopes containing their holiday details.

Max was very excited about his cheap adventure surprise. The next week both Max and Max opened their sealed envelopes containing their destinations. They left the house in two taxis and travelled their separate ways.

Max did not enjoy his cheap adventure surprise. It was much cheaper than he expected! He had no blanket for his bed and no cup for his drink. The hotel even locked him in his room!

Once Max returned from his holiday, he called his travel agent to complain.

"Hello?" answered the travel agent.

"This is Max!" yelled Max.

"Hello, Max. How was the surprise holiday cruise?" asked the travel agent.

"The c—c—cruise…?"

Max hung up immediately and realized that he had made a big mistake.

He had stayed in a kennel! And Max, the dog, had enjoyed his surprise cruise!

The Vanishing Invention!

"I've done it!" yelled the inventor. "I'm a genius! I'm the smartest inventor in the world!" he screamed in his laboratory. He ran from his laboratory onto the street.

"Look everyone! I have made something incredible!" the inventor declared to the world.

"Oooooh," said everyone in the street. "What is it? Can we see it?"

"Actually, the idea is you that you cannot not see it! I'll show you!" replied the inventor. "Ta-da! I present to you my new invention, the Smarty Pants! No more checking pockets for things in your pants, now you can see what is in them!"

The inventor pressed a button on his watch.

Suddenly, the street went silent. No one made a sound. Everyone stood still staring at the inventor.

It was very awkward.

Then they stared anywhere but at the inventor. Everyone could absolutely see what was in his pants. Because his pants turned invisible! The inventor stood proud in his underwear with a big grin on his face. **"I'm going to be famous!"**

The Funny Fairy Tale!

Once upon a time, in a faraway land, in the woods, in a cottage, there lived a husband and wife. They were old and had always wanted children, but they never had any children.

They would take walks through the forest every afternoon.

One day, they were walking down the same path they took every day. All of a sudden the wife pointed and said to her husband, "Look! What's that?"

Her husband looked and answered, "It's a basket! And there's a baby inside!"

The couple was very happy. They had found a baby who had been left in the woods. Now they could take care of this baby just like it was their own.

They took the baby home and gave him a bath. They were feeding him some carrot soup when something very strange happened.

The baby burped and all of a sudden he wasn't a baby. He had changed into a lizard!

There was now a baby-sized lizard in a diaper sitting in front of the couple!

"Oh no!" shouted the husband. "What's wrong with this baby? Babies don't normally burp then change into baby-sized lizards, do they?"

"I don't think so," answered the wife.

The lizard slurped up some more carrot soup, then it burped and suddenly turned back into a baby!

"Don't worry," the wife said to her husband. "It's a baby again."

The next day, the husband and wife were eating breakfast outside with the baby. The baby refused to eat his pea and onion soup, and he was crawling around the garden.

The couple had planted all sorts of food in their garden—turnips, potatoes, tomatoes, pears and pineapples. The baby crawled past all of these and found the carrots growing in the garden.

He pulled one out and began to eat it.

The husband and wife heard a huge burp, and the baby changed into a camel!

"Oh dear!" the wife said to her husband. "The baby has changed into a camel now. I don't think babies are supposed to change into camels."

They watched as the camel ate some more carrot then suddenly changed back into a baby.

"Hmmm…" the husband said. "I think I have an idea…"

The next day, the husband told his wife that they should celebrate the baby's birthday.

"But we don't know when his birthday is," the wife said.

"That's okay," he replied. "We'll just make today his birthday. Let's bake him a cake—a carrot cake!"

The wife agreed, and they made a big carrot cake for the baby's birthday. They sang "Happy Birthday," and the baby blew out the candles. The husband cut the cake and gave every family member a slice.

Within three seconds, the baby had eaten his cake. He gave a loud burp and changed into a dolphin!

"It's happened again," the wife said to her husband. "Now the baby's turned into a dolphin! Why does he keep changing into things? That doesn't seem normal for a baby!"

"I figured it out!" the husband exclaimed. "Whenever the baby eats anything with carrots, he burps. When he burps, he turns into an animal! He then turns back into a baby when he eats more carrots and burps again. We found a magical baby in the woods!"

"Oh dear," the wife replied. "We got a broken baby. But I love him so much. Can we keep him, husband?"

Just then, there was a knock on the door. The husband opened the door and found a big, ugly, mean troll outside.

"What are you doing here, you big, ugly, mean troll?" the husband asked. "Get out of here and go back to the woods where you belong!"

The husband and wife tried to chase the troll out of their garden.

The troll roared back, "You have something that belongs to me! That baby is mine! I found him first! I just left him in the woods for a few minutes, and you stole him from me. I was going to eat him for dinner! Instead, all I had to eat were some Brussels sprouts! Yuck!!"

The troll was running straight for them now, but the husband had an idea. He pulled a carrot out of the garden and gave it to the baby. The baby ate the carrot and loudly burped. He turned into a worm!

The troll laughed and snatched the worm away. "Ha ha! What are you going to do with this? Silly humans!"

The husband and wife held each other, shaking with fear. What could they do now?

But the worm still had some carrot. It ate a small piece and burped, turning back into a baby.

"Thank you, baby," the troll said. "You look much tastier now than you did as a worm!"

The wife didn't want to see her baby eaten by a troll. How could she rescue him from the hands of the troll? She decided it was worth one more try! She quickly threw another piece of carrot to the baby. The baby ate it and burped, and this time he turned into a whale!

The troll screamed. He couldn't hold up a whale. The whale crushed him! The husband and wife ran up to the whale, which was still sitting on the troll. They hugged him and kissed him.

"This is the best baby ever!" the husband and wife said to each other.

They gave the whale a carrot and it changed back to a baby. And that was the last carrot the husband and wife ever gave the baby.

The Dodgy Doctor!

Jim ran to the doctor in a great hurry.

"Doctor help me!" pled Jim.

"What is it?" asked the doctor.

"While completing my homework I fell asleep at my desk," explained Jim slowly. "And...," he continued, "I was chewing on a pencil."

"Hmmm," the doctor said nodding.

"Well..., I swallowed my pencil!"

The doctor paused, then reached into his desk drawer.

"Here, take this," the doctor said as he was passing something to Jim.

"Thanks, doctor. What is it?"

"It's an *eraser*."

Another Funny Fairy Tale!

Fairyland was full of talented creatures. But no one knew who was the most talented, so the creatures of Fairyland held a talent show.

It was decided that the troll would be the judge. He was grumpy, and he did not want to enter the contest. Also, the troll always told the truth. If you were bad, he would let you know!

The Fairyland creatures practiced and practiced their acts for the big show. Everyone was very excited.

Well, everyone except for Debbie the unicorn.

She didn't know what her talent could be. She was nervous, and her voice always broke into a neigh, so she knew she couldn't sing. She was clumsy and always tripping over her four hooves, so she knew she couldn't dance. Her hooves didn't have fingers, so she knew she couldn't play the trumpet. She wasn't very funny, so she knew she couldn't tell jokes. What could she do?

Debbie thought and she thought and she thought, but she couldn't think of anything she could do for the talent show.

Finally, it was the day of the talent show. Debbie still had no ideas for her act. She decided to sit in the audience until it was her turn on stage, hoping to think of an idea soon.

The first contestant was the Fairy Godmother. She sang a beautiful song while she tap-danced on stage. Everyone in the crowd stood up, clapping.

Debbie thought to herself, "Wow, it's going to be tough to beat her! What can I do that's better than that?"

The next contestant was an ogre. He got up on stage and did impersonations. First, he pretended to be a knight riding on a horse. Everyone laughed. Then, he pretended to be a giant stomping on houses and eating people. Everyone screamed in terror. For his last impersonation, he pretended to be a dragon. He flapped his arms like wings and blew his bad breath into the crowd like fire. Everyone in the front row passed out from the stench. The troll judge seemed to really like this trick!

Debbie thought to herself again, "Wow, that ogre was really good! What can I do that's better than that?"

The next contestant was a mermaid. She hopped up on the stage with a basket full of tennis balls. She sat down and she hit the tennis balls with her tail into the crowd. One even hit a dwarf right in the eye!

"Wow, what a great shot!" Debbie thought to herself. "But what can I do that's better than that?"

Next, a witch flew onto the stage. She performed a bunch of magic tricks. First, she made a castle disappear. Then, she made a goat talk and tell jokes. For her last magic trick, she turned the other contestants into sugary bread dough!

She laughed with a big, loud cackle. She thought she had gotten rid of all of the contestants with her trick! She thought she had won the talent show!

The troll judge stood up and cleared his throat. "Well..." he said. "It seems that the witch has cheated. She will lose 75 points from her score. But, because the other contestants have been turned into sugary bread dough, she is winning the talent contest with 25 points. Are there any other talent show contestants? Or will the witch win the talent show?"

Debbie cleared her throat and began to speak softly. "Um, excuse me, Mr. Troll," she said. "I also signed up for the talent show, but... um... I'm still trying to decide what my talent is."

The troll judge frowned. "Well, we don't have all day!" he shouted. "Either get up on stage or give up and sit back down! And will someone move those bread dough contestants out of the way?"

Debbie knew she couldn't give up. She had to get on stage. She was so nervous that she was trembling. And when Debbie got nervous, she became clumsy!

"You can do this," she said to herself. "Just don't trip on the stage in front of everyone. Don't trip. Don't trip. Don't trip…"

Debbie tripped! She stumbled off the stage!

Luckily, something squishy broke her fall. She opened her eyes and saw that her unicorn horn had cut through the dough contestants!

"Oh no!" Debbie thought. "What did I do? How embarrassing!"

Debbie turned bright red. She was blushing. She could feel the heat from her embarrassment all over her head.

But something smelt strange. Her face was burning so much from her blushing that it was cooking the dough!

Debbie stood still, too embarrassed to move.

The troll judge walked up to her and pulled a piece of the dough off her horn. It still had the hole in it where her horn had pierced through. He took a bite, then smiled and began clapping.

"This is the best thing I've ever eaten!" he shouted.

Everyone else in the audience rushed around Debbie. They each took a piece with a hole in it.

"Yummy, that's delicious!" they shouted, one after another.

The troll judged shushed everyone until they were quiet. "I hereby declare that Debbie the unicorn is the winner of the talent contest! She magically created these delicious morsels of dough with holes in the middle. No one in Fairyland is more talented than Debbie!"

And that's how Debbie the unicorn invented the first doughnuts!

The Vikings!

Dark clouds filled the sky. Lightning crashed on the sea, and thunder echoed through the air. The wind became stronger, and the waves became larger.

"This storm is going to sink our ship!" shouted Erik the Viking. "Quick, steer the ship towards that island! It's the only way to save the ship!"

The Vikings battled the storm and were able to make it to land.

"We'll spend the night by the beach and explore the land tomorrow," said Erik.

The Vikings quickly made shelter to escape the storm and went to sleep. The next morning, they woke up early, ready to explore the new island.

Erik led them over a hill and across a stream. There was not a single person on the whole island. Finally, they found a large valley and the only living things on the island.

The valley was full of bulls and cows. Erik and the other Vikings were amazed. They'd never seen animals like these!

One of the Vikings went up to a bull. "Look!" he shouted to his friends. "This one has horns just like the ones on our helmets!"

The other Vikings approached some of the other bulls. They felt the horns on the bulls' heads and they felt the horns on their helmets. They were just alike! The Vikings were so excited!

"Their horns are so beautiful!" one of the Vikings shouted.

"I really love their horns!" another Viking shouted.

The Vikings loved the bulls' horns so much that they soon began to love the bulls, too.

The bulls on the island found this weird. After a short time, the bulls were annoyed by all the attention the Vikings were giving them. The Vikings would sing all day and night to the bulls. Finally, the bulls had enough of the Vikings' attention. One night the bulls snuck onto the Vikings' ship with the cows and sailed away.

The End

Printed in Great Britain
by Amazon